Bob Hartman

Cheer Up, Chicken!

For Caitlin

Cheer Up, Chicken!

Bob Hartman

Illustrations by
Mike Spoor

Gregory was an old man. He lived all by himself in the forest, with only the foxes and the bears for his companions. But he was not lonely, for he spent his days praying and tending his tiny garden and growing close to God and the world that God had made.

And so it was that he grew wise. And the people who lived in the city would travel for days to find him, and talk with him, and discover the answers to the mysteries of life.

"Father Gregory," said a visitor one day. "You are so thin and frail. Why, I can count the bones through your skin. Take this gift, I beg you. It will do you good."

And the man handed Gregory a chicken.

"What a wonderful surprise!" Gregory exclaimed. "Thank you so much for this generous gift."

Then he put the chicken on the ground, and went back to his prayers.

When the time came for dinner, Gregory looked at the chicken. And the chicken looked at him.

Gregory dreamed of how good that chicken would taste, cooked with onions and a few small carrots.

The chicken dreamed of how good it would be to gobble down a few bits of grain.

But before either of their dreams could come true, Gregory dreamed another dream.

He dreamed of a friend, a young tinker, who had been ill recently. Surely he needed the chicken much more than Gregory?

So, right then and there, Gregory tucked the chicken under his arm, and set off to find his friend.

He walked all night and half the next day. The chicken had never been so frightened!

"Cheer up, chicken!" Gregory smiled. "No harm will come to us." And the old man was right—the foxes and the bears paid him no heed, and the sun shone cheerfully through the branches.

At last he knocked on his friend's front door.

"Cachoo!" sneezed the tinker. "Come in."

"I cannot stay," Gregory apologized, "but I thought this might help you through your illness."

And he handed the chicken to the tinker.

"What a thoughtful thing to do," the tinker sniffled. "Thank you so much for your kindness."

Then he put the chicken on the floor, and went back to bed.

When the time came for dinner, the tinker looked at the chicken. And the chicken looked at him.

The tinker dreamed of how nice that chicken would taste, boiled down to a rich steamy broth.

The chicken dreamed of how nice it would be to scratch around at the ground again.

But before either of their dreams could come true, the tinker dreamed another dream. He dreamed of a girl, far off in the city, whose little dog had died.

"That child is lonely," he thought. "She misses her little dog. Surely she could use this chicken more than me?"

So, right then and there, the tinker tucked the chicken under his arm, gave his nose a good blow, and set off for the city.

He walked for one day, for two days, for three days, sneezing and coughing all the way. The chicken had never been so bored!

"Cheer up, chicken!" the tinker sniffed. "We'll soon be there."

At last the tinker knocked at the little girl's door.

"Cachoo! I'm sorry to disturb you. I mended some pots
for your parents recently. They told me about your little
dog. I hope that this will help."

And he handed the chicken to the girl.

"A chicken!" the little girl shouted. "A chicken of my
very own. I will love her and take care of her always.
Thank you so much!"

Then she put the chicken on the floor, and ran to tell
her mother.

When she got back, she looked at the chicken. And the chicken looked at her.

The little girl dreamed of how wonderful it would be to hug the chicken and take it for walks, and teach it to do little tricks.

The chicken dreamed of how wonderful it would be to sit on a nest of eggs and raise a little family.

But before either of their dreams could come true,
the little girl dreamed another dream. She dreamed
of a poor beggar woman she had seen in the street
that day.

"That woman has no food or friends," she
thought. "This chicken could keep her company
and give her eggs every day."

So, right then and there, she put a ribbon around the chicken's neck, tied two bows on its legs, and set off to give her beautiful bird to the beggar woman. The chicken had never been so embarrassed!

"Cheer up, chicken!" the little girl smiled. "There's somebody I want you to meet."

They walked down wide streets and narrow alleys, through crowded markets and empty squares. At last, the little girl found the woman, sleeping in a heap against a tall dark wall.

"Wake up!" the little girl called. "Wake up, please."

The beggar woman grunted and shook and snored. Then she gave the girl a drowsy stare.

"Here," said the little girl," I thought you might like this." And she handed the chicken to the woman.

"Why, thank you," yawned the woman. "No one has ever given me a gift as beautiful as this before." And her sweet sleepy smile made the little girl glad.

The beggar woman put the chicken on the ground, tied the ribbon to her belt, and fell right back to sleep.

When she awoke, the woman looked at the chicken. And the chicken looked at her.

The woman dreamed of what she could get by trading the chicken at the market.

The chicken dreamed of farms and fields and wide open spaces.

But before either of these dreams could come true, the beggar woman dreamed another dream. She dreamed of a man who had helped her once, many years ago.

"Perhaps," she thought, "he could use this chicken even more than me?"

So, right then and there, she tucked the chicken under her arm, hitched a ride on a pedlar's wagon, and set off to find her old friend.

The ride was bumpy. The ride was rough. The chicken had never been so thrown about!

"Cheer up, chicken!" the woman grinned. "You'll soon have a brand new home."

At last they arrived. The beggar woman slid off the wagon and hurried to her old friend's house.

"Well, there you are," she said. "It's good to see you
after all these years. But how you've changed. Maybe this
will fatten you up."

And she handed the chicken to… Gregory!

"What a wonderful surprise!" Gregory grinned.
"It is good to see you, too. And to be the object of your
generosity."

Then he bid farewell to the woman, but he did not put
the chicken on the ground.

No, Gregory looked at the chicken long and hard.
And the chicken looked at Gregory.

"We've met before, my friend, haven't we?" the old man chuckled.

The chicken said nothing, of course. But she couldn't help wondering what would happen now.

"Someone gave you to me. I gave you to the tinker. Here you are, back again. And only you know how many others there have been in between. I say it's time for your travelling to end."

At those words, the chicken dreamed an awful dream— a dream of gravy and carrots and stew.

But before her dream could come true, Gregory
opened his door and shooed her out into his garden.

"Cheer up, chicken!" he said. "We shall spend what's
left of our days together, scratching around in this tiny
garden."

And so it was that each one gave,
each one received, and all were blessed.
And no one more than the chicken!

Text copyright © 1998 Bob Hartman
Illustrations copyright © 1998 Mike Spoor
This edition copyright © 1998 Lion Publishing

The moral rights of the author and artist
have been asserted

Published by
Lion Publishing plc
Sandy Lane West, Oxford, England
ISBN 0 7459 3725 X
Lion Publishing
4050 Lee Vance View, Colorado Springs, CO 80918, USA
ISBN 0 7459 3725 X

First edition 1998
10 9 8 7 6 5 4 3 2 1 0

A catalogue record for this book is available
from the British Library

Library of Congress CIP data applied for

Printed and bound in Belgium